THE LAND OF DREAMS

Created & Written by: Kathleen Michael
Illustrations by: Laurie Edwards & Kathleen Michael

All songs written by: K.Michael & J. Michael
All songs published by Krissy Tunes BMI

Background Vocals by: Patricia D'Angelo
Musicians: R. McCormick, J. Michael

Produced by: J. Michael / Michael Entertainment Inc.

P.O. Box 160052, Nashville, TN 37216
e-mail: www.krissybook@aol.com

Library of Congress Cataloging-in-Publication Data. The Land of Dreams. (Krissy Books) summary: Krissy overcomes the fear of shadows in the dark when going to sleep at night. (Fiction)

Manufactured in the United States of America.

Krissy always loved going to school.
Her teacher, Miss Nickie, was very nice.
She even let the class help choose the
rules they would be following.

Some of the children had trouble keeping these rules, but Krissy was happy to please Miss Nickie and obey her. She liked it when Miss Nickie said she was a good student and it made her feel so proud when she saw her pictures on the wall for open house. Krissy was learning to read and write, add and subtract, all those grown-up things, but she couldn't wait for school to be out, so she could begin to play.

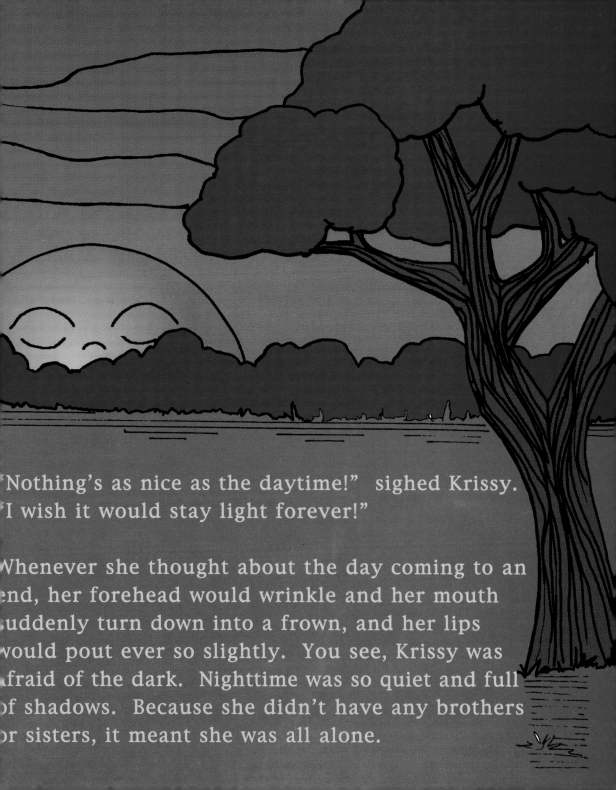

"Nothing's as nice as the daytime!" sighed Krissy.
"I wish it would stay light forever!"

Whenever she thought about the day coming to an
end, her forehead would wrinkle and her mouth
suddenly turn down into a frown, and her lips
would pout ever so slightly. You see, Krissy was
afraid of the dark. Nighttime was so quiet and full
of shadows. Because she didn't have any brothers
or sisters, it meant she was all alone.

Each night, after she had her bath, she would coax her Mother or Father into reading her a story and sitting in bed. They would talk about Krissy's day, and then they would pray together.

"Father God, please take care of Mommy and Daddy. Help my friends at school to obey Miss Nickie, and please make the sun shine at night!" Krissy prayed.

"Krissy, God won't make the sun shine at night. He can't disobey His own rules for night and day, but if you ask Him, He will help you not to be afraid of the dark." Mother said.

After prayers were over, Mother looked at her watch and said, "Enough is enough! No more books, no more toys, no more stories. It's time to get quiet and go to sleep. Give me a kiss and I'll turn out the light. It's past your bedtime, again!"

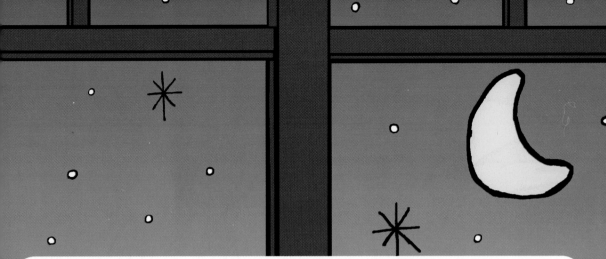

"But Mother," Krissy pleaded, "I don't want you to go. I will be all alone. The shadows still scare me and I'm afraid to close my eyes."

"Oh, Krissy," sighed Mother, "those shadows can't hurt you. Besides, your Father and I are just in the next room. Now, settle down and go to sleep. It will be morning before you know it."

Mother left and, after a while, Krissy heard them turn off the TV and go to their room.

"Good-night, Daddy," shouted Krissy!

"Good-night, sweetheart. Come snuggle with us in the morning."

Krissy tried to go to sleep, but it was just too hard. Oh, how she wished bedtime could be fun.

"If I had a sister to share my room, I wouldn't be scared. Mother has Daddy. If only I had someone-- someone just for me."

Tears were falling as she started to cry, when, all of a sudden, she heard a soft gentle voice. Hovering at the foot of her bed was a fluffy pink little cloud.

Krissy had never had so much fun. She opened
her eyes thinking she would still be floating
around the land of dreams, but instead she saw
the familiar things that were in her room, and
heard her Mother calling,

"Krissy, wake up now! If you don't get a move
on it you'll be late for school.

Krissy hurried to get ready, her mind racing
with the memory of the dream. Was it just a
dream? Did she really make friends with a cloud?
But the question most on her mind...would she
ever see her little cloud again?

For the first time in her life, Krissy found it hard to keep her mind on her school work, and play time passed by so slowly, Krissy began to wonder if the sun would ever set.

Finally, as it began to get dark, Krissy hurried through her supper, had her bath, and was in her pajamas before her bedtime.

She kissed her Mother, then her Father, and went to bed without the usual story, books and all the other excuses she used to stay up late.

As soon as Krissy said her prayers, she closed her eyes. She wouldn't fight the urge to go to sleep tonight, and she wasn't afraid of the shadows. She was too excited. She wanted to be with her new friend.

She didn't think she'd ever fall asleep and was just
about to get up and go to her mother when she heard
the soft voice of her friend,
"Hi, looking for me?" he gently asked.
"Where did you go last night? I opened my eyes and
you were gone. I didn't know if I would ever see you
again!"
Krissy's eyes filled with tears.

"I had to leave," replied the cloud. "During the day I have a job to do. I water the trees and flowers and fill the rivers, lakes and streams. I often provide shade from the sun."

Krissy thought about the fun she always had walking in the rain and splashing in the puddles. She was glad that the cloud had important things to do during the day, because she didn't want to miss her friends at school or the time she had to play.

"At the end of the day, Krissy, I got very lonesome.
My job was done and I would have to let some of the
other clouds have their turn. But I'm so small, tha
in the dark most of the other clouds didn't even
notice me. One night I heard you crying because
you were all alone. So I came to see you. Now I
have a night time friend."

"Then you'll be here every night?" Krissy asked anxiously. "When you're here I'm not afraid."

"All you have to do is go to sleep and think of me." he said. "You're my friend, and I'll always come to you."

From that day on, Krissy didn't need anybody telling her when it was time for bed. She looked forward each night to being with the pink cloud in her dreams.